THE TIMEKEEPERS

Eiffel Tower Emergency

Contents

Chapter 1

Tickets for two

"Hey, look at this!" Hannah's dad called as he came back from the orchards. "The peaches are ripening perfectly. Catch!"

She caught the peach he tossed her. It was firm and fuzzy, and warm from the sun.

Hannah was sitting in the shade of the veranda that went right around her home. She'd lived on the family's farm in New Jersey, on the east coast of the USA, all her life. She always loved being outside, where the summer breeze carried the sweet scent of peaches.

Her worktable was covered with newspaper to keep it clean. A lot of painting, cutting, and gluing happened here. Hannah had built a model skyscraper using lolly sticks and cardboard, and her next task was to paint people on small squares of plastic that she'd cut from used food packaging. They would make great windows.

"I'll have my very own skyscraper in the countryside," Hannah said to herself, as she lifted the peach to her mouth. She was about to take a bite when she noticed that the hands on her special watch were spinning.

She felt a thrill of excitement. Time for an adventure!

Hannah was a member of the Timekeepers, a secret organisation with members from all over the world. A villain called DeLay loved to mess around with time, trying to make history go wrong. It was the Timekeepers' task to travel into the past and make sure that history happened the way it was supposed to.

What's DeLay up to now? Hannah wondered, as she flipped open the watch face. She pressed one of the buttons inside. Instantly, the hands whizzed faster and faster, and everything around her froze. The leaves on the trees were still, the birdsong fell silent, and a pair of blue speckled butterflies stopped in mid-flutter.

A rainbow whirl surrounded Hannah. She felt herself rising from her seat as the swirling colours turned bright white. No one would see her go, and she knew no one would worry about her while she was gone, because time stayed still while she was away.

The next moment, she felt her feet touch the ground. The white light faded, and she found herself in a wonderful museum. It was full of shelves and display cases which were crammed with historical objects, from a tiny Roman glass bead, to a silk robe worn by a baby prince in the 18th century.

This was the History Hub, the headquarters of the Timekeepers.

"Hannah here!" she called.

She heard a rustling sound and looked up at a large cuckoo clock on the wall. Hannah guessed that the cuckoo inside was climbing out of her nest. Sure enough, the clock's little red door opened, and a bright-eyed bird popped its head out.

"Hello, Tempo!" said Hannah.

"Cuckoo!"

"It's lovely to see you too," Hannah said, as Tempo flew down onto her shoulder with happy little squawks.

The little bird was great friends with the Timekeepers, and was involved with all of their adventures.

In a sudden flash of white light, the next Timekeeper arrived.

"Sarah here!" said a girl who wore a pretty pink headscarf. "Hi, Hannah! Hi, Tempo! Just jotting down a new story idea," she added, scribbling in her notebook. Sarah adored writing!

Tempo flew up to the little ledge outside her red door to watch the other arrivals.

Flash!

Flash!

Two boys arrived almost together. One wore a shirt patterned with sea creatures. "Luke here!" he called.

"New shirt?" asked Hannah, knowing he'd made it himself. Luke was mad about fashion. "It looks great!" she said when Luke nodded enthusiastically.

"Kingsley here!" sang the other boy, who was a brilliant musician. His favourite guitar was slung over his shoulder.

Flash!

"Rosa here!" said a girl in a tracksuit. She had her football boots tied together, hanging around her neck.

Flash! Flash!

Two more Timekeepers arrived at the same time.

"Min-Jun here!"

"Jackson here!"

Min-Jun had a tube of glue and a tiny paintbrush in his top pocket, so Hannah guessed he'd been working on one of the miniature figurines he loved making. "Mmm, something smells delicious," Min-Jun said.

Jackson laughed. "That'll be me! I've been baking jam tarts," he said. He adored cooking.

Flash!

"Yasmin here!" She looked as if she'd been hurrying. "Am I last? I was trying a new piece of code on my computer. It worked!"

An empty glass display case stood in the middle of the History Hub. As the Timekeepers gathered around it, there was a flash inside the case, and two pieces

of thin card appeared. Rosa opened the
latch and took them out.

"They're tickets for the *Exposition
Universelle*," she read. "I wonder what
that means?"

"I know," said Hannah. "We've been
studying French history at school. The
Exposition was a World Fair, with lots
of exhibitions for people to come and
look at. It was held in Paris in the
19th century."

"Ooh," said Kingsley.
"Someone's off on a Parisian
adventure. But who?"

The Timekeepers looked up
at Tempo.

The cuckoo took off and flew
around the room, then perched

on Hannah's shoulder.

"I've been chosen!" she said with a grin of delight. "Who's coming with me?"

Tempo circled the room again and landed on Jackson's shoulder.

"I'm going with Hannah!" he cried. "Wow! France!" Jackson's New Zealand home was on the other side of the world, far from Europe.

"You'll need these," said Rosa, handing the tickets to Hannah. "I can't wait to hear about what you see at the World Fair!"

The Timekeepers flipped open their watches to reveal hidden screens.

"We'll be standing by," said Luke. "Ready to give you any help you need."

"Thanks," said Hannah. "Between us, we'll put a stop to whatever trouble DeLay's cooking up."

Tempo flew around Hannah and Jackson, faster and faster, until a wall of brilliant white light surrounded them. Hannah's feet lifted off the floor, and the next moment, the light vanished, and she and Jackson were standing on firm ground.

Hannah was now facing a wide river, which teemed with boats of all sizes. People walking along the towpath called to each other in French, and she could

hear clanging and banging, as if a lot of building was going on.

"That must be the River Seine, which runs through Paris," she said to Jackson. He was facing the other way – and his mouth was hanging open in amazement. Hannah spun round to see what he was looking at.

It was a tall, red-brown, metal structure, standing on four great legs. It was made of thousands of iron beams, and it rose high up into the air.

"The Eiffel Tower!" she breathed.

Chapter 2

The perfect patisserie

"Cuck-OO!" Tempo flew off over the River Seine. She loved exploring new places, just as much as the Timekeepers.

Hannah flipped open her watch. The screen said they had arrived in Paris in 1889. Her trainers were gone. Now she wore black ankle boots, fastened with

tiny buttons. Instead of jeans and a jumper, she wore a cherry-red jacket and matching skirt, which had layers of petticoats underneath to make it stick out.

Jackson's brown boots and long red socks were topped by blue trousers ending just below his knees. He had a stripy jacket and a straw hat. He grinned. "This is *not* what I usually wear."

"The History Hub always gives us the perfect outfits so that we fit in," said Hannah. "I like your gold jacket buttons."

"They're a bit fancy," Jackson said. He grinned cheekily. "I like your hat."

"*What?*" Hannah reached up to find a red beret perched on top of her head. "Oh, this is very French, I like it."

They had satchels over their shoulders, so they checked inside to see what they'd been given.

"I've got tickets, pencils and a notebook," said Hannah. "And there's a paper bag of sultanas in the front pocket — Tempo's favourite treat!"

"I've just got a notebook and pencils," said Jackson.

"If we've got time, I might sketch the

Eiffel Tower," Hannah said, gazing up at the massive construction. Its criss-crossing beams reminded her of the lattice top that her parents put on peach pies, using strips of pastry. She'd seen the tower loads of times in books and movies, but now she was seeing it for real. Except…

"It doesn't look right," she said, as Tempo returned to her shoulder. The tower rose high above everything else, but… "Of course!" Hannah exclaimed. "It's not finished. The top's missing!"

Tempo made a noise like a cross between a squawk and a cackle.

"What was that squackle sound about?" Hannah asked, tickling the bird's head.

"I think she's telling us to go and look around!" Jackson said, pointing to a board saying 'Admission' – the French word for 'Entrance'. Painted on it was an arrow pointing beneath the Eiffel Tower.

"Good idea, Tempo! Maybe we'll find DeLay and discover what our mission is," Hannah said.

"Hmm, though it looks like the fair's not open yet," Jackson said as they got closer to the tower. "See? It's just people with tools and carts going through."

"We can try to sneak in," Hannah

said eagerly. "Maybe they won't notice us."

Jackson laughed. "With a cuckoo on your shoulder?"

"Maybe I can coax her into my bag." Hannah stroked Tempo's chest and said, "Would you like a tasty treat?"

Her grey head bobbed. "Cuck-er-uck-oooo!"

"She's definitely feeling peckish!" said Jackson.

Hannah helped Tempo to snuggle inside her satchel. Leaving the bag's flap open, she tucked in a few plump sultanas.

They walked past the kiosk, but a man with a droopy moustache told them, "We're not open yet. Only workers and officials can go in. And journalists, of course."

Hannah didn't miss a beat, and immediately whipped out her notebook. Flipping it open, she said, "We're journalists for the…er…The *Tempo Times* newspaper. We've come to report on the preparations."

The man eyed them suspiciously. Hannah smiled, hoping she looked confident. Now she knew why the Hub had provided them with notebooks and pencils.

"You're rather young to be journalists," the man said. "But in you go."

"That was quick thinking," Jackson whispered to her once they were through.

"Thanks," Hannah said. She led Jackson through, thinking, *phew!*

An avenue with lawns laid out in rectangles and circles stretched ahead of the Timekeepers. Fountains lined a long pool in the middle, and a magnificent building stood beyond that. It had a gold dome, topped by a winged figure. Bright white statues stood across the front.

"This isn't like the fairs I go to in New Zealand," Jackson said. "Where are the rides?"

"This isn't just any fair," said Hannah. "The World Fairs were displays of different countries' culture and technology. Some of them had rides, but not all of them!"

Jackson looked back at the Eiffel Tower. "So that's being built especially for this fair?" he assumed. "They certainly are going to a lot of trouble for it."

On either side of the avenue, men in blue jackets were working on long low buildings, so the Timekeepers turned down a path with houses that looked like they came from all over the world. Jackson pointed out a white one with a flat roof and small windows. "That one looks Egyptian," he said. "Seems like it might help keep people cool in the hot desert."

Hannah liked a house on their left which had two roofs that tipped upwards at the corners. "I think this one's Chinese!"

As they were deciding where to go next, a smoky smell wafted over to them.

Jackson sniffed. "Something's burning," he said. "It smells like it does when I've burned a tray of biscuits."

A wail echoed from a food stand that looked like a little cottage. It was on the end of a row of empty kiosks by the tower. A sign hanging above told them it was called, 'The Perfect Patisserie'. A big front window was the serving hatch, and the Timekeepers could see someone inside, flapping a cloth at the billowing smoke.

Jackson raced over. "Let's make sure no one's hurt!" he called back. Hannah dashed after him and they burst through the side door.

A girl who looked about their age
stood clutching a cloth and staring at a
tray of burned pastries.

"Are you okay?" Hannah asked.

The girl shook her head. "I'm
confused," she said. "I only just put these
in the oven, and now they're *black*... How
could they burn so quickly?"

She noticed another tray of pastries on a shelf. "Oh no!" she shrieked. "I put those out to cool only a moment ago. Look at them now!"

The pastries were covered with mould.

The Timekeepers shared a glance. They had a good idea what had caused this.

"That's awful," Hannah said. "My name's Hannah, by the way." She nudged Jackson, who was peering at the burned pastries.

"Sorry," he said. "I'm Jackson." He leaned over to examine the mouldy ones.

"My name's Suzette," said

the girl. "My whole morning's work is wasted. I can't bear to start all over again."

Jackson straightened up. "Suzette, I love how artistic your pastries are. See, Hannah?"

The pastries were shaped like little Eiffel Towers.

"They're so clever!" said Hannah. "Visitors to the fair will love them!"

"Thanks." Suzette gave a small smile. "You've made me feel better. I need to make money to help my family, so I'll get back to work."

The Timekeepers left her weighing flour.

"DeLay's behind Suzette's troubles," Hannah said, as they walked along a path edged with scented yellow roses.

"Definitely," said Jackson. "Suzette's cakes and pastries are ruined, maybe he's thrown a Time Crunch."

Time Crunches were nasty little devices that looked like pocket watches. DeLay used them to cause glitches in time. They made **tick tick tick** sounds before erupting into a cloud of smoke. They were able to speed time up, or slow it down, and they always caused trouble.

Hannah nodded. "At least it's proof

that DeLay's around here somewhere."

Just ahead, a group of people were holding notebooks and had gathered around a low platform.

"They look like journalists," said Hannah. "Let's see what they're here for. Perhaps it's something to do with our mission."

Holding their own notebooks, they joined the group.

"Hello, Mademoiselle," said one of the men. "Playing journalists, are you?"

How rude! thought Hannah. "Actually, we *are* journalists," she said. "My parents

own a newspaper."

"Sorry, Miss," the man mumbled.

Another journalist with a moustache like a hairy caterpillar said, "Here comes Monsieur Eiffel!"

Jackson nudged Hannah. "Fibber," he whispered. "Your parents don't own a newspaper."

"They do," Hannah said with a mischievous grin. "Dad bought one with his coffee just this morning!"

Jackson chuckled just as Hannah nudged him to look over at the platform. A man with a neat, pointed beard, had just stepped onto it.

"Bonjour, everyone! Good day!" he said, removing his top hat. He smoothed his thick, wavy hair. "I'm Gustave Eiffel, and workers from my engineering company are building this tower. It's a pleasure to show their achievement to you, so you can write about it in your newspapers. When the tower's finished, it will be just over 312 metres high – the tallest structure in the world!

"Excuse me, Monsieur," said the man with the caterpillar moustache. "Do you think anyone will ever build anything taller than that?"

Gustave Eiffel smiled. "For now, my tower is record-breaking," he said, "but one day I think people will make buildings that are even higher. Maybe people will live in them – imagine that!

When you write about the tower, please say what an amazing feat of engineering it is, and that it's already being used for scientific experiments and measuring wind effects. It will have a weather station at the top, too. Come! I'll give you a tour."

The Timekeepers followed the group, amusing themselves by naming some of the tall buildings that would one day be built.

"New York's Empire State Building," said Hannah.

"New Zealand's Sky Tower," said Jackson.

"The Shard in London," Hannah added. "I bet the Eiffel Tower inspired the engineers that worked on all of those skyscrapers."

Gustave Eiffel halted beside one of the tower's legs and gestured to some stairs that headed upwards inside the structure. "Welcome," he said, "to the gem of Paris, the star of the World Fair, and the greatest work of my life – the Eiffel Tower!"

Chapter 3

The top of the tower

Hannah and Jackson followed
Monsieur Eiffel and the journalists up the
spiral staircase. Above them rose the metal
beams of the tower.

"The lifts aren't working yet,"
Monsieur Eiffel explained, as they went
up. "But believe me, it's worth walking up

all of these stairs for the view at the top!"

"How many stairs are there?" Jackson asked.

"There will be 1,665 when the tower's finished," said Monsieur Eiffel. "The lifts will be ready in a few weeks. An American company's installing them. They've demonstrated that if you cut the cable that holds the lift, it would stop before hitting the ground. They call them 'safety elevators'. Marvellous invention."

Monsieur Eiffel stopped so the group could admire the view. Hannah showed Jackson places she'd learned about in school: the Arc de Triomphe, the Champs Élysées, the Louvre Museum, and of course the River Seine, which was snaking through the city.

Monsieur Eiffel patted a metal beam. "It's taking 7,300 tonnes of iron to build my tower, and over 18,000 metal parts," he said, and smiled. "Its nickname is the Iron Lady."

"Sir, how are the beams fixed together?" Hannah asked.

"Good question!" he replied. "We use cylinder-shaped pieces of iron, called rivets, to fix two beams together. The rivets are heated, then put through holes in the beams where they are to be joined. Then the ends are hammered flat so the rivet can't fall out."

"Why do they heat them?" asked Jackson.

"Another good question!" Monsieur Eiffel looked delighted. "When the rivet cools down, it shrinks a little, which pulls the beams together even more tightly. It's simple, but it works."

When they reached the first level, they stopped again.

"I can see for miles," said Jackson.

"You can look down on all the palaces and pavilions of the fair too, as well as at all the people," said Monsieur Eiffel. "It's like being a bird!"

Inside Hannah's satchel, Tempo gave a little cuckoo.

Monsieur Eiffel showed them four grand restaurants, one on each side of the level. "We'll also have refreshment kiosks and a patisserie," he said. "Something for everyone!"

As they set off again, a journalist,

who looked rather pale, said he was going back down. "I've never been up this high," he said as he headed for the stairs. "I don't like it. Suppose the tower were to fall?"

A tall man asked nervously, "*Could* it fall?"

Monsieur Eiffel smiled. "No. My engineers are the best. We plan to be open to visitors for the next twenty years!"

"Hmmm," said a journalist, "maybe the people of Paris won't want to look at it for another twenty years…"

Gustave Eiffel glanced around the group. "I know that some people think it's ugly," he said. "I think it's magnificent, and I'm sure that most people will come to appreciate its strange beauty. They'll miss it when it's taken down."

Hannah grinned at Jackson. Nobody would miss it because it wouldn't be taken down. It was impossible to think of Paris without the Eiffel Tower – even in the 21st century!

The journalist with the bushy brown beard edged forward. He wore a hat pulled well down, and a baggy raincoat the colour of wet sand. It had a short cape around the shoulders and a belt tied around the middle.

The journalist spoke in a husky voice. "Where is your office, Monsieur?"

"In my apartment, on the

44

top level," Monsieur Eiffel replied.

"Is that where you keep the plans for the tower?" the bearded journalist asked.

Monsieur Eiffel smiled patiently. "It is."

"I see," the bearded man said. "Does your apartment have a good view?"

Monsieur Eiffel relaxed. "Of course," he said. "There's a window, and a balcony all the way around."

"Wonderful!" said the bearded man. "I'm looking forward to seeing it."

"Then up we go!" said Monsieur Eiffel, beaming at them all. Hannah checked that Tempo was still snoozing in her satchel, then followed the group. By the time they reached the second level, two more journalists – who looked a little green from the height – decided they couldn't climb any higher.

"I'm sure you'll feel better if you take a look at the printing works we're setting up on this level," Monsieur Eiffel said to them. "There'll be a special newspaper printed here every day."

The rest of the group continued. Halfway to the top, Hannah shaded her eyes and squinted into the horizon. The view was wonderful – she could see the countryside around Paris now. Far into the distance, there were two tall steeples, which looked tiny and faint in the hazy sunlight. "Monsieur Eiffel," she said, pointing. "I can see a church or cathedral with two towers – one taller than the other?"

"Young eyes!" he said. "I can only see it from the top, but I'm sure you're describing Chartres Cathedral. It's 56 miles from here."

Hannah and Jackson grinned. What a view!

They pressed on, and eventually Monsieur Eiffel stopped by a door and produced a key from around his neck. "Welcome to my apartment," he said.

They entered a room furnished with a desk, bookshelves, lamps, a carpet, and comfortable armchairs. Hannah and Jackson sank into them, and so did several of the journalists.

"Let me show you an activity we've got planned that will be fun for visitors," Monsieur Eiffel said as he opened a cupboard and rummaged inside. He emerged from the cupboard holding a tiny parachute. "Visitors will be able to write a postcard, attach it to a parachute like this, and launch it from the top of the tower. Who knows where the wind might carry it?"

Hannah spotted something familiar on a shelf – a statuette of a woman, holding a flaming torch high in the air.

"That's the Statue of Liberty from New York!" she said. "Why do you have it, Monsieur Eiffel?"

"Please, call me Gustave," he said. "I have it for three reasons. One, it's beautiful. Two, it's a symbol of freedom and justice. And three, I designed the metal framework the statue is built around! I don't have the original plans for it here, I'm afraid, but you might like to see the plans of my tower?"

"Yes, please!" said the Timekeepers.

He went to a side table and then began to look confused. "Now where…?"

Hannah asked, "What's wrong, Gustave?"

"M–my plans," he said slowly. "They were rolled up, right here. They've gone!" He pushed journalists aside as he rushed around, opening drawers and looking in cupboards. "They were tied with red, white, and blue ribbon! Where are they?"

Jackson said quietly to Hannah, "Someone else has gone too."

She glanced around. The bearded journalist was nowhere to be seen.

Hannah and Jackson's eyes met. They spoke together. "He's DeLay!"

Chapter 4

Stolen!

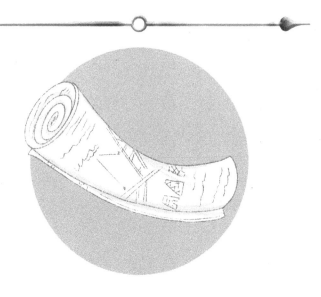

The Timekeepers ran out of the room. Out on the platform again, Hannah became more aware of how high up they were. She focussed her eyes on the stairs so that she didn't get dizzy.

Jackson was already heading downwards, but Hannah was soon close

behind him. "We know it's you, DeLay!"
she shouted to the bearded figure
that sprinted ahead of them, his long
coat flapping.

"Cuckoo!" Tempo called, as she shot
out of Hannah's satchel and swooped
after DeLay.

Jackson managed to run at full speed and grab DeLay's coat belt, but the villain wriggled out of his coat entirely and left the Timekeepers stumbling over it. The jacket he wore underneath was styled with a pocket watch pattern.

"Ha, nice try!" DeLay said as he flung his false beard at them.

Hannah spotted a roll of paper sticking out of his jacket.

"Give back those plans!" she yelled.

DeLay slowed. For a moment, Hannah thought he was going to do as she said. But no, DeLay's hands were busy with something. Tempo flew at him, flapping her wings in his face. He batted her away and launched a little parachute out between the iron beams.

What's he up to? Hannah wondered. She leaned out to see…and gasped. Dangling beneath the slowly drifting parachute were the plans. She could clearly see the red, white, and blue ribbon tied around them.

DeLay screeched with laughter and hurtled down the stairs again, spiralling around and around.

Tempo flew to Hannah. "Cuckoo?" she squawked.

"Yes, Tempo!" cried Hannah. "After those plans!"

The cuckoo zoomed out of the tower, while the Timekeepers tried desperately to catch DeLay before he did any more damage.

Hannah's legs were wobbly, but she pounded on down the stairs. Though they'd run down hundreds of steps, they were still quite high up.

DeLay, a flight ahead of them, fished something from his pocket.

"Look out, Jackson!" Hannah called. "It's a Time Crunch! He'll throw it back to slow us down."

But instead, DeLay
flung the Time Crunch a
few steps ahead of himself.
It rolled down the stairs,
but Hannah could still hear
its **tick tick tick**.

DeLay tore after it, like a wasp
chasing an ice cream van. It burst into
smoke just as he reached it, and vanished.
The Time Crunch had sped up time
around him so he could move
super-fast. Chasing him was pointless.
He'd escaped.

The Timekeepers slowly climbed
all the way back to Gustave's
apartment. They found the engineer
in a terrible panic.

"What am I going to do?" he groaned. "We can't finish the tower without those plans. It's a disaster!"

One of the remaining journalists said to the other, "We always thought the tower would be a failure, didn't we, Pierre?"

"We did, Claude," said Pierre. "Seems we were right."

Hannah turned to them. "It will not be a failure," she said fiercely. "Jackson and I will find those plans. You'll see!"

Gustave grasped Hannah's hands. "Thank you," he said. "Both of you. No one has ever built a tower so tall. If it fails, maybe no one will have the confidence to try again. For the sake of progress, and for the success of the World

Fair, this tower *must* be finished!"

The Timekeepers promised Gustave that they would not let him down, and as the journalists headed for the stairs, Hannah and Jackson beat them to it. They galloped down them and heard Gustave call, "*Bonne chance!* Good luck, my young friends!"

Back on the ground, the Timekeepers spotted Tempo perched on an empty cart in the shade of the tower. The little bird launched into the air with a loud, "Cuckoo!" then fluttered in place.

"**Cuck000!**" she called again.

"I think she wants us to follow," said Hannah.

Tempo led them to the side of 'The Perfect Patisserie' and fluttered to the ground beside a torn parachute.

"This must be where the plans landed," said Jackson.

"Cuckoo!" Tempo bobbed her head up and down.

Hannah stroked her. "Well done," she said. "But where are the plans?"

Suzette appeared with a small bowl of water and a large strawberry. "Your bird is so sweet," she said, putting them down for Tempo. "I found her guarding the parachute."

"Thanks, Suzette," said Hannah. "A roll of papers was attached to the parachute. Do you know what happened to it?"

"Yes, I saw them," Suzette nodded. "A strange-looking person whizzed from the tower at top speed and snatched them."

"That's DeLay," Jackson told her. "Those were Monsieur Eiffel's papers."

"Are they important?" Suzette asked.

"*Vitally* important," Hannah replied.

"Monsieur Eiffel can't complete the tower in time without them – and DeLay is trying to stop him. The tower *must* be a success. It's the fair's star attraction!"

Suzette buried her face in her hands. "Why didn't I grab the papers when I had the chance?" she said. "Who will want Eiffel Tower pastries if the tower is a failure? Our family patisserie struggles enough as it is. You're right. It *has* to succeed."

Hannah realised that many people, like Suzette, were depending on the tower's success.

"Don't worry," she said. "The tower *will* be completed, and it *will* be a success."

"So will you, Suzette," said Jackson. "I'm sure people will love your pastries."

Suzette smiled gratefully. "Did you see where the thief went?" Hannah asked her.

"Yes, he pushed the postman off his bike and stole it!" said Suzette. "Then he cycled down the fair's main avenue."

They said goodbye to Suzette, and Tempo flew over to gently fluff a wing against the young French girl's face. "Cuckoo," she said softly.

Suzette waved the Timekeepers off with a brave smile. Hannah and Jackson hurried past partially built stands, and decorators painting their countries' exhibition pavilions. Everywhere Hannah looked, there was something different to see. Some of the pavilions, such as the

Venezuelan one, were very fancy, with
curly plasterwork, but others, like the
Indian one, were simple and elegant.

In one area, large paintings were
being carried into the Palace of Fine Art.
Hannah was so distracted by them that
she almost fell over a man who was
sprawled face-down on the ground. Three
large rectangular packages wrapped in
brown paper lay beside him.

She knelt by the man. "Are you
okay?" she asked.

"I think so," he said, as Jackson
helped him sit up.

The man wiped dust from his
moustache and pushed a lock of curly
hair back from his forehead. He reached
for one of his packages. The paper was
torn off the corner, and Hannah glimpsed
a painting inside. He stood slowly. "I was
bringing my paintings to the Palace of
Fine Art when a cyclist in a very odd
jacket sped past at an incredible speed
and sent me flying."

"I'm very sorry to hear that," Hannah said. "Did you paint these?" she asked, pointing to the wrapped artwork.

"I did," he said. "My name's Edvard. Edvard Munch, from Norway."

Hannah stared in thrilled surprise. This man was famous! Practically everyone would recognise a painting of his, known as 'The Scream'. There was even an emoji that looked like it.

If only I had time to talk to him!

"We're trying to stop the cyclist who knocked you over. Did you see where he went?" Jackson asked.

"Yes," Edvard said, pointing down the street. "He went that way!"

Chapter 5

Help from the hub

Hannah ran down the street, just behind Jackson. She nearly crashed into him when he suddenly stopped.

"What's up?" she said.

He sniffed the air. "Smoke."

"Not again!" said Hannah.

Jackson shook his head. "Not burning food," he said. "Not that sort of smoke."

Hannah sniffed too. "Hmm. It smells like…"

"A Time Crunch!" said Jackson. He pointed to a wooden box on a nearby wall. It was roughly the size and shape of a letterbox. "See that? It's got wisps of smoke hanging around it."

"So, DeLay was here," said Hannah. "But why? Let's see what's so interesting about that box."

They peered at it. A black object stuck out from the front. It looked like something you might speak into. On the side was a hook with another black object hanging on it. That one was connected to the box by a wire.

"I think it's an early sort of phone," Hannah said. "You hold the bit on the side to your ear and speak into the front bit."

Jackson rubbed some dust away. "It's got the word 'Bell' on the front," he said, "but I can't see one. Why was DeLay so interested in it?"

"Let's try it," said Hannah. She picked up the side piece and put it to her ear. "Do I just speak?" she asked. "Or should I press something?"

The earpiece suddenly crackled, and a voice said, "Hello, losers."

It was DeLay!

Jackson took one look at Hannah's face and leaned in closer to listen.

"I do so enjoy our chats. It would have taken those buffoonish workers all day to install that phone, but thanks to my Time Crunch they did it in a blink. You two must think you're so clever," DeLay taunted them, "but you're never as clever as me. And I just wanted to tell you that you won't ever get those plans back!" He snorted with laughter, and, with a click, he was gone.

Jackson's eyes lit up. "Hannah, there were hardly any phones in this time. But if DeLay can speak to us, he must be somewhere where they have another one. If we can find it, we'll find DeLay – and the plans. But where could it be?"

"We'll call the History Hub," Hannah decided, "and ask the other Timekeepers if they can find out." She glanced around. No one was near, so she and Jackson flipped open their watches. A gallery of friendly faces appeared on the screens.

"How can we help?" asked Min-Jun.

Hannah quickly explained what had happened, while Jackson held up his watch to show them the telephone.

"If we want to find DeLay and the plans, we need to do it quickly," Hannah

told them. "But there isn't time to search every building for another phone."

"We're on it," said Sarah. "That box telephone was invented by Alexander Graham Bell over ten years before your World Fair. In 1889, not many people had ever seen one."

"Oh, *that's* why it has 'Bell' written on it," said Jackson.

Yasmin spoke up. "I'm sending a map of the fair to everyone's screens."

They all pored over it, then Luke gave a shout and zoomed in to a building, labelled, "Telephone and Electricity Pavilion."

"That must be where DeLay called from," said Rosa.

Hannah checked its location. "It's quite close," she said.

"I'll leave the map on your screens," Yasmin said, "so it's there if you need it."

"Thanks, everyone," said Hannah. "Wish us luck! Bye!"

With Tempo flying overhead, the Timekeepers sprinted to a building with huge windows, and flags fluttering above the roof. They slipped inside, where a man was rolling up cables and stacking them in a box. He was surrounded by heaps of tangled wires.

"Mind you don't trip," he said.

They stepped carefully towards him. "We're looking for a rather peculiar person, wearing a suit with pocket watches all over it," Jackson said.

The man laughed. "I'm not likely to forget him! He was here when I got back from my break," he said. "He was using the telephone, though we're not ready for visitors yet. I sent him away."

Hannah thanked the man then turned to Jackson. "I really hoped we'd find DeLay here."

"We'll catch him," said Jackson. "Timekeepers never give up, remember!"

"I know," said Hannah. "Let's think. We know DeLay knocked over Edvard

Munch's paintings. We know he messed around with the Bell telephone. We know he's trying to spoil the Eiffel Tower. He seems to target famous and important things – inventions and artworks."

She examined the map again and touched the 'Flip' icon by mistake. The map turned over.

"'List of exhibitors'," she read. A familiar name jumped out at her. "Thomas Edison!" she cried.

"Huh? What about him?" asked Jackson.

"He was a great inventor," said Hannah. "He worked on light bulbs, the movie camera, the phonograph—"

"The what?" Jackson looked puzzled.

"The phonograph – an early sort of

music player. Edison's inventions are just the sort of things DeLay would mess around with."

Jackson jumped up. "We'd better find him then. Where shall we look?"

Hannah stabbed the map with her finger. "Here!" she said. "The Palace of Machines!"

Chapter 6

Time crunch trail

The Palace of Machines was the biggest building the Timekeepers had come across. It was made of iron, steel, and huge panes of glass. On the sides of the building, they saw things that looked like huge arched conservatories.

Music was playing when they entered, and Tempo immediately joined in.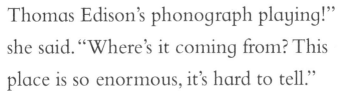

"**Cuck-er-uck-er-uck-er-ooo**," she squawked.

Jackson laughed, and Hannah felt a thrill of excitement. "That must be Thomas Edison's phonograph playing!" she said. "Where's it coming from? This place is so enormous, it's hard to tell."

The centre aisle sat between all sorts of machines, engines, and gadgets. "I wonder what they all are?" Hannah was saying, when a man with a tin of paint and a brush called out from the top of a ladder.

"Hey you, down there!" he shouted.

"The Palace of Machines is open to visitors!"

"We're journalists looking for Thomas Edison," Jackson said. He had to cup his hands around his mouth to be heard.

"Journalists, eh?" the man said. "Alright then." He pointed upwards to what looked like a giant tray on wheels fitted onto railings. "Louis will sort you out."

"What on earth is *that?*" Hannah asked. The contraption's rails ran high above the exhibits.

"That's the best way to get to Edison," the man said. "We call it the rolling bridge. There's room for about thirty people on that, I reckon. Louis is the driver. Hey Louis!" he called. "Some

passengers for you. Journalists!"

The Timekeepers climbed a stairway and stepped onto the rolling bridge. Louis pulled a long handle, releasing the brake, and they started to move.

The lovely music they'd heard suddenly sped up.

"What a racket!" Louis said.

Jackson whispered, "DeLay!"

Hannah nodded. The villain was obviously affecting the speed of the music.

Seconds later, the music slowed to a growl.

"That's even worse," said Louis.

"Cuck-ook-ook-ooo!" Tempo squawked.

Looking down, Hannah saw a smart man wearing a bow tie, and with neatly combed hair. He was staring at a big box with a brass trumpet shape attached to it. Was that the phonograph?

That must be Thomas Edison!

"Louis!" Hannah cried. "Stop at the next stairs, please."

Moments later they were back on the ground floor. They found Mr Edison frantically fiddling with the box. He glanced up, looking worried sick.

"Something's not right," he muttered to himself. "My phonograph was fine earlier. What if I can't fix it in time for the fair? It's a disaster! This invention means people won't need to go to a concert hall to hear music, they can listen to it – *in their own sitting rooms*! Imagine! But now everything's going wrong."

"There's someone running around the fair causing trouble," Hannah said. "I think he's to blame for the issues with your phonograph. He's wearing a jacket with a pocket watch pattern. Have you seen him?"

Mr Edison looked grim. "I certainly have." He pointed over Hannah's shoulder. "Right there!"

The Timekeepers turned and gasped.

DeLay was halfway down the long aisle, leaning against a shiny machine covered with switches and dials. He had a smug look on his bony face.

"Don't worry, Mr Edison," Hannah said. "We'll fix this."

Tempo swooped ahead as they raced towards DeLay.

We've got you, Hannah thought.

But DeLay reached into his pocket and flung something down by his feet.

Tick tick tick!

A Time Crunch! As it burst into smoke, DeLay sped up.

"Faster, Jackson!" Hannah panted. "We have to get those plans!"

Tick tick tick!

They stopped. "Another Time

Crunch!" said Jackson, as smoke billowed in front of them.

"Stay clear of it!" cried Hannah. "It will slow us down."

They nipped between two large engine-like contraptions and ran outside, tracking DeLay by following the puffs of smoke. The last one was in the entrance to another building. The sign said, 'Palace of Food Products'.

Inside, the air was filled with the aromas of chocolate, spices, coffee, herbs, gingerbread, oranges, garlic, and many other delicious smells. People were putting finishing touches to elaborate food displays on rows of long tables or individual stands.

A complicated structure of ladders was being used to build a massive pyramid of different types of melon. Hannah wondered what would happen if someone removed one of the striped melons at the base of the pyramid.

Everywhere the Timekeepers looked, there was something extraordinary: giant biscuits, a wedding cake with eleven tiers, and a statue of a woman with no arms, made entirely of chocolate. It was labelled 'Venus de Milo'.

They passed a Leaning Tower of Pisa, also sculpted from chocolate. Jackson frowned and peered closely at it. "It's starting to melt."

A fishy smell greeted them at the next stand, where lobsters and crabs crawled around a huge tank. As the Timekeepers passed a pen containing clucking hens, they found another chocolate statue – a woman singing with her arms held wide.

"Yuck! Look at her hands," Hannah said.

The singer's fingers were melting. They were twice as long as normal and hung from her hands like bats dangling from a tree.

"DeLay is going to spoil everything in this place!" said Jackson.

They hurried on past a chocolate sculpture of the Arc de Triomphe. Its runny chocolate was starting to spread across the floor.

Suddenly, their path was blocked by the smirking figure of DeLay.

"Can't stop me," he jeered. "I'm always ahead of you. You'll never get these plans." He waved the roll of papers at them, then dodged behind a big stand which was being stacked with jars. The sign said: 'Henry Heinz's Pickles'.

"Hey, this is my stand," said the man. Hannah assumed it was Henry Heinz himself. "Go away!"

DeLay heaved the whole thing over, sending pickle jars tumbling to the floor. Some smashed, but lots rolled towards Hannah and Jackson.

"Watch out!" cried Mr Heinz.

The Timekeepers leapt clear as DeLay sauntered away, whistling.

Mr Heinz shook his fist. "You scoundrel!" he cried. "You've wrecked my exhibit!"

Hannah and Jackson started picking up the rolling jars, but Mr Heinz said, "Thanks, I'll fix it. You make sure that villain doesn't damage anything else. He's probably ruined my business."

The Timekeepers ran off. The man was upset, but Hannah was confident he'd be all right. Mr Heinz's company was world-famous in her time.

DeLay had vanished. Hannah and Jackson went into a side section of the palace, and found a huge arch made of stacked chocolate bars that reached almost to the ceiling. A sign said there were 250,000 bars in the stack!

"Wow! I could make quite a few cakes using that lot," Jackson was saying, when a voice called from behind the chocolate bars.

"Yoo hoo!"

The Timekeepers ran through the arch to see DeLay running up a steep ramp and leaping onto a gigantic barrel of lemonade. He pulled the hatch off the top and dangled Gustave Eiffel's plans, still tied with red, white, and blue ribbon, directly above the opening.

"DeLay, don't!" Hannah cried.

"There's nothing you can do, losers," he cackled. "I'm going to drop them in the barrel. So take a last look before they're destroyed – forever!"

Chapter 7

Chocolate and cream

Tempo dived at DeLay.

She flapped her wings in his face,

forcing him backwards.

"Get away!" He lashed at her with a

bony hand.

But Tempo circled the villain's head

and squawked in his ears.

DeLay drew his arm back and swiped at Tempo with the roll of plans, as if it was a baseball bat.

The clever cuckoo dodged him easily, but DeLay toppled backwards, off the barrel. He landed on the ramp.

Thud!

"Ooof! Oww! Yeow!" DeLay rolled over and over, all the way down the ramp.

He finished up flat on his back at the foot of a tall tower made of chocolate éclairs. The long pastries were filled with thick cream and topped with shiny chocolate icing. They reminded Hannah of her model skyscraper – she'd had to stack the lolly sticks very carefully, to stop the skyscraper falling over.

Maybe this éclair tower could help save the Eiffel Tower…

DeLay was still distracted, trying to swat the cuckoo away.

"Keep him busy, Tempo!" Hannah cried. "Jackson, do what I do!"

She darted to the side of the tower of éclairs where DeLay was lying, and began pulling them out from the bottom of the stack. Jackson joined her, flinging cream-filled éclairs over his shoulder.

Once they'd made a big hole in
the side of the tower, it started leaning
towards them. It wobbled and leaned
a bit more.

"Tempo, move away now!"
Hannah cried.

DeLay was now alone, still on his
back. He looked up just in time to see the
tower topple.

"Nooooo!" he cried and reached for
a Time Crunch. He was too late.

Splat!

Thlop!

Thlump!

The villain was buried under a huge heap of pastry, soft cream, and squidgy chocolate.

"Hooray!" cried Jackson.

Hannah needed to do something before she could raise a cheer.

She stepped around the other side of the gooey mess and saw a bony hand sticking out. It was clutching the plans. She edged forward carefully, but her feet were sliding in the creamy gloop, and she had to go back.

"I can't reach them," she groaned.

"Cuckoo!" Tempo flew down, grabbed the red, white, and blue ribbon in her beak and pulled the plans out of DeLay's hand. She dropped them into Hannah's arms. "Cuck-OOOooo!" she cheered.

"Good work, Tempo!" Hannah said. She leapt back as DeLay struggled to the surface. He was covered in creamy chocolate sludge and looked *very* cross.

"This isn't the last you've seen of me," he snarled as he wriggled free.

Thlump!

Another load of éclairs landed on his head.

"We'll be watching for you," Hannah said.

Jackson nodded. "And we'll never let you get away with changing history."

"Cuck-uck-uck-uck-oo!" squawked Tempo.

"Pah!" said DeLay. "I'll be back!" And, in a puff of dirty grey smoke, he was gone.

There were cries from the main part of the building.

"Smoke!"

"Something's burning!"

As Hannah wiped blobs of cream from the plans, a crowd gathered.

"It's all right," Jackson told them. "There's no fire."

A man in a baker's hat groaned. "My éclairs...! What happened?"

Henry Heinz spoke up. "I'm not exactly sure, but from what I've seen and heard, I have a feeling the World Fair has been saved by these two young people and their clever bird."

"Cuckoo!" Tempo fluffed her feathers proudly.

"Sorry to leave you with such a mess," said Hannah. "I have to take these plans to Monsieur Eiffel."

"I'll catch you up, Hannah," said Jackson. "I'm going to stay and help with the éclairs. I could mix a fresh batch of pastry."

The baker smiled. "*Fantastique!* Let's do it!"

Hannah and Tempo made their way back to the foot of the Eiffel Tower, where they found Gustave. He was approaching anyone who passed by and asking if they'd seen a roll of paper tied with red, white, and blue ribbon.

"Yes," said a woman. She pointed to Hannah. "It's right there!"

Gustave turned. He beamed in delight. "My dear young friend! You said you'd find my plans, and you have! How can I ever thank you?"

Hannah smiled. "Just finish your tower, Gustave," she said. "Then whenever I look at the very top, I'll remember meeting you!"

Chapter 8

Postcard from Paris

Hannah and Tempo caught up with Jackson after he'd successfully helped the baker with his éclair tower. Jackson brought a couple of the sweet treats for them to try. Tempo pecked at some of the chocolate icing and gave a happy chirp.

As Hannah lifted the last morsel to

her mouth, her eye was caught by her watch. The hands were moving!

"Check your watch, Jackson," she said.

He looked down at his wrist. "The hands are spinning," he said, "but forwards, not backwards!"

Before Hannah could reply, they were surrounded by a flash of bright white light. When it cleared, she found they were in the middle of a crowd of excited, chatting people. Most of them were looking upwards, amazed by the height of the tower above them.

Hannah and Jackson looked up too and gasped in delighted surprise. The Eiffel Tower was complete. They'd gone forward in time!

"Gustave finished it," said Hannah. She felt proud that he'd only managed it because she and Jackson had saved his plans. "Let's go up and see him," she suggested.

"Okay," said Jackson, "but let's get another snack on the way. I'm smelling delicious smells and they're making me hungry."

"Cuckoo!" Tempo clacked her beak a few times.

Hannah laughed. "Tempo's hungry again, too!"

They showed their tickets at the kiosk, then climbed the stairs to the first floor. As Jackson looked around at the food kiosks, he moved aside to let a girl with a tray of pastries pass.

Hannah recognised her. "Suzette?"

The girl turned. "Hannah! Jackson!" she cried. "And Tempo!"

"Cuckoo!"

Hannah laughed. "We're all pleased to see you," she said. They hugged her carefully, so she didn't tip her tray.

"Why are you up here?" Hannah asked.

Suzette beamed. "The patisserie people here asked me to supply them with my Eiffel Tower pastries," she said. "They're very popular, so they're sold up here as well as in The Perfect Patisserie. My family will be fine now, and it's thanks to you for saving Monsieur Eiffel's plans."

She gave them each a tiny Eiffel Tower-shaped pastry, which they nibbled as they climbed upwards. It was late, and lights were twinkling all over Paris. The palaces and pavilions far below glittered with light too, and illuminated fountains sparkled in the dark.

Thousands of gas lamps were lighting the tower. The Timekeepers glanced up through the ironwork lattice and saw a

beacon at the top, shining red, white, and blue – the colours of the French flag.

"It's so beautiful," Hannah breathed.

When they reached Gustave's door and had got their breath back, Hannah knocked. "Enter," said a voice, and they went in to find him at his desk.

He jumped up. "My friends!" he said, grasping their hands. "It's good to see you once more. Thank you again for finding my plans! My tower is beautiful, yes?"

"Yes!" said Jackson.

"Very beautiful!" added Hannah.

Gustave rubbed his hands together. "The lifts will be in action soon, then it will be easy for everyone to explore the tower. Please excuse me for a moment."

He went to his desk and wrote on a postcard. Then he took a little parachute from a drawer and attached the postcard to it. He went out onto the balcony and released it.

Hannah and Jackson watched the postcard float away into the night.

"Is the postcard for your family?" Hannah asked.

Gustave smiled and shook his head. They chatted for a while, then the Timekeepers said goodbye and left him to his work. "*Au revoir*," Gustave replied.

"And thank you!"

Hannah closed the door behind them. "It's time to go home," she said.

"Mmm, back to my jam tarts," said Jackson. "Though I won't be eating any just yet. I'm still full of éclair and the Eiffel Tower – Suzette's Eiffel Tower!"

"Cuckoo!" Tempo flew around their heads, circling faster and faster until there was only white light. In moments, Hannah and Jackson were back in the History Hub, in their own clothes, surrounded by the other Timekeepers.

"Congratulations!" Sarah, Yasmin, and Kingsley said together.

Min-Jun clapped them on the back. "You did it!"

Rosa was about to speak when Luke said, "Hannah! Behind you!"

She spun around and could scarcely believe what she was seeing. A little parachute was drifting across the History Hub. Dangling below was a postcard.

Hannah caught it and read it aloud:

From the Eiffel Tower, Paris, 1889.

Dear Hannah and Jackson, this message comes to you from the top of the tower that you saved. You are brave and clever, and I am so grateful to you. I hope you receive this postcard. I feel sure you will – eventually.

Yours truly, G. Eiffel

Gustave Eiffel

P.S. Please give my regards to the amazing Tempo.

"Fantastic!" said Yasmin. "I'll pin it on the Moments in Time noticeboard with the postcards from our other missions."

It was time to say goodbye. "We'll see each other soon," said Hannah. "Thanks, everyone, for your help! And thank you,

Jackson, for sharing the mission…and for the éclair!" She pressed a button on her watch and, after a final "Bye!", dazzling light surrounded her.

There she was, back on her veranda, with her skyscraper waiting to be painted. And there was her peach, fuzzy and warm, and deliciously scented.

That amazing adventure has given me an idea! Hannah thought.

She fetched a string of battery-powered fairy lights from her bedroom. She lowered them onto her skyscraper and switched them on.

"There!" Hannah said to herself, as she bit into the peach. "Tonight, my skyscraper will look almost as beautiful as the Eiffel Tower!"

The
EIFFEL TOWER

The Eiffel Tower was built for the Exposition Universelle, or World Fair, in 1889, which celebrated the 100th anniversary of the French Revolution. It is now one of the most well-known landmarks in the world, and has almost seven million visitors every year.

Prepared in advance
A lot of the rivets (metal bolts that hold the tower together) were inserted in advance at a factory. This, alongside steam cranes and lots of workers, allowed the tower to be built quickly.

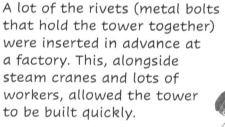

Built in two years, two months, and five days, the Eiffel Tower's construction was very speedy and impressive.

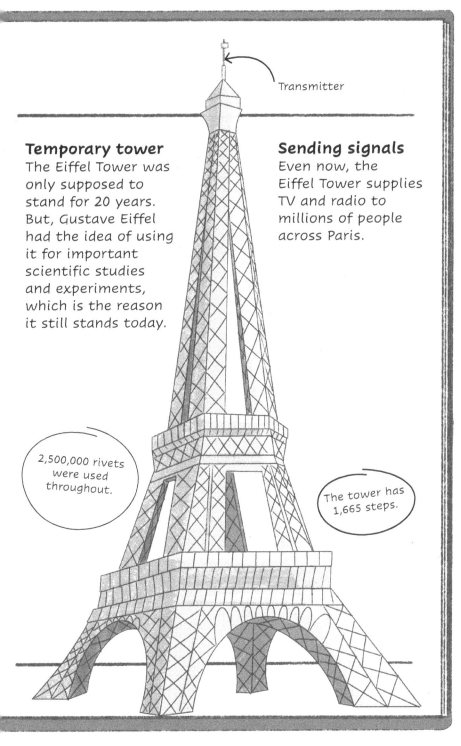

Transmitter

Temporary tower
The Eiffel Tower was only supposed to stand for 20 years. But, Gustave Eiffel had the idea of using it for important scientific studies and experiments, which is the reason it still stands today.

Sending signals
Even now, the Eiffel Tower supplies TV and radio to millions of people across Paris.

2,500,000 rivets were used throughout.

The tower has 1,665 steps.

Gustave
EIFFEL

Gustave Eiffel was born in 1832 in the French city of Dijon. He was an engineer and entrepreneur, who was nicknamed the "magician of iron" for his impressive work building metal structures.

Early life

After studying chemistry in Paris, Eiffel was hired by an engineer who specialised in steam-powered machines and railways. Eiffel constructed many of France's national railways, and led the building of a now-famous railway bridge. The bridge was his first great achievement, and earned him recognition.

Eiffel's first masterpiece:
Passerelle Eiffel, Bordeaux, 1860

Garabit Viaduct, 1885

G. Eiffel and Co.
Eiffel founded a company in 1867 which constructed viaducts, railways, road bridges, and large buildings with metal frames.

Supporting Lady Liberty
Eiffel also designed the steel framework to support the weight of the Statue of Liberty, a gift from France to the USA in 1885.

Eiffel built the first aerodynamic laboratory, where he worked throughout WWI.

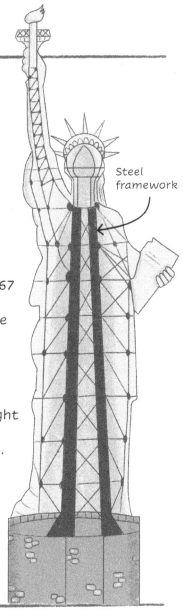
Steel framework

World
FAIRS

World Fairs are international exhibitions designed to showcase nations' cultural, industrial, and scientific achievements. They are usually held for three to six months. The first was held in Prague, in what is now Czechia, in 1791.

In 1851, London's Crystal Palace was built to host their "Great Exhibition".

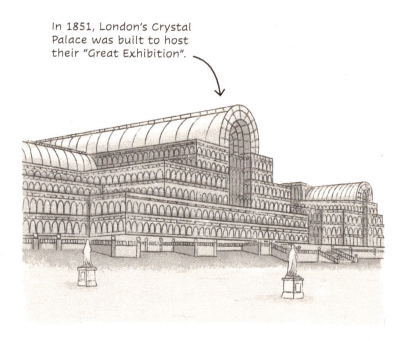

The golden age

The 'golden age of world fairs', took place between 1880 and 1914. More than 40 international expositions were held in a variety of locations, including the USA, Australia, Guatemala, and French Indochina (now Vietnam).

France's world fairs

The first French world fair was held in 1855. It lost money, but left a positive legacy, and the French government sponsored many more fairs, each with more attendees. The world fair in 1889, for which the Eiffel Tower was specifically built, attracted more than 32 million visitors!

121

Quiz

1: True or false: Time stands still while the Timekeepers are on a mission.

2: Hannah and Jackson pretend to be journalists to enter the World Fair. What newspaper do they say they work for?

3: Which of Thomas Edison's inventions did DeLay try to damage?

4: True or false: The Eiffel Tower was completed in 1989.

5: Which French landmark do the Timekeepers see sculpted from chocolate?

6: Who built the Eiffel Tower?

7: True or false: Edvard Munch's famous painting is called 'The Shout'.

Glossary

Aromas
Strong, but pleasant smells.

Beacon
A light in a high place that signals, warns, or guides people and vehicles.

Buffoonish
Clown-like, foolish, stupid, or ridiculous.

Contraption
A machine or other device that looks complicated, strange, old-fashioned, or is difficult to use.

Elaborate
Detailed, and often beautifully designed.

Engineering
A type of science that involves building and designing machines and structures.

Illuminated
Lit up.

Jeered
Shouted rudely.

Kiosk
An open-fronted area where information is given, or items and tickets are sold.

Lattice

A diagonal crisscross pattern or structure.

Morsel
A small piece of something, often food.

Patisserie
A shop which sells pastries and cakes.

Pavilion

A temporary structure which displays items at exhibitions.

Phonograph

The first machine that could record sound and play it back.

Time crunch

A magic device used by DeLay to control the flow of time.

Time travel

The ability to travel back and forward in time to visit the past or future.

Veranda

A covered platform attached to the outside of a building.

Quiz Answers

1. True

2. *The Tempo Times*

3. The phonograph

4. False – it was completed in 1889

5. The Arc de Triomphe

6. Gustave Eiffel

7. False – it is called 'The Scream'

Penguin
Random
House

For the eagle-eyed Liz Wilding.

Text for DK by Working Partners Ltd
9 Kingsway, London WC2B 6XF
With special thanks to Valerie Wilding

Design by Collaborate Ltd
Illustrator Esther Hernando
Consultant Anita Ganeri
Acquisitions Editor James Mitchem
Editor Becca Arlington
Designer Ann Cannings
Jacket and Sales Material Coordinator Magda Pszuk
Senior Production Editor Dragana Puvavic
Senior Production Controller Inderjit Bhullar
Publishing Director Sarah Larter

First published in Great Britain in 2024 by
Dorling Kindersley Limited
One Embassy Gardens, 8 Viaduct Gardens,
London, SW11 7BW

A CIP catalogue record for this book
is available from the British Library.
ISBN: 978-0-2415-5915-4

Printed and bound in Great Britain by
Clays Ltd, Elcograf S.p.A.

www.dk.com

The publisher would like to thank Kate Sayer for picture library assistance.